For my great friend Lorna and her beautiful daughters. C.W.

For my delightfully noisy nibblers, Lori and Jamie. R.B.

First published in Great Britain in 2013 by Andersen Press Ltd.,
20 Vauxhall Bridge Road, London SW1V 2SA.
Published in Australia by Random House Australia Pty.,
Level 3, 100 Pacific Highway, North Sydney, NSW 2060.
Text copyright © Carrie Weston, 2013. Illustration copyright © Richard Byrne, 2013.

Printed and bound in Malaysia by Tien Wah Press.

10 9 8 7 6 5 4 3 2 1

British Library Cataloguing in Publication Data available.

ISBN 978 1 84939 559 5

MIX
Paper from responsible sources
FSC® C012700

What Noise Does a Rabbit Make?

Written by **Carrie Weston**

Illustrated by **Richard Byrne**

ANDERSEN PRESS

In the still of the night,
just before dawn,
slowly and silently . . .

. . . the meadow filled
with rabbits.

Raggety-Taggle
   and his brothers
      and his sisters,
         his aunts,
            and his uncles,
               all nibbled peacefully.

But as the sun came up . . .

Cock-a-doodle-do!

trumpeted the cockerel.

Moo!

went the cows.

Neigh!

said the horses.

Baa-baaaaaaaaa!

the sheep joined in.

Oink! Oink!

grunted the pigs.

Tweet
Tweet

Meow!

went the cat in search
of her breakfast.

Woof!
Woof!

barked the dog as the farmer
started his tractor.

Chu-chu-brrr-chug,
chug, chug!

The farm rang out with noises.

Raggety-Taggle listened with his long ears and thought very hard.

Tweet Tweet

"Just what noise **does** a rabbit make?"

he wondered.

Raggety-Taggle tapped
his foot and thought.

Thump - thump -
thumpety-thump.

A long way off,
in the tall grass,
two ears pricked up.
A tail flicked.

Two eyes blinked.

Whiskers twitched.
The cat licked her lips.

Thump - thump -
thumpety - thump!

went Raggety-Taggle.

He didn't see that
the other rabbits had
swiftly, silently,
disappeared into their burrows.

The cat crouched.
The cat wriggled.

The cat . . .

MIAOW!
Hiss!

Raggety-Taggle
ran
for
his
life.

Through the cow field,

Mooo ooooO oooooo!

over the sheep pen,

Baa-baaaa!

round the stables,

Neeeeeeeigh!

under the pigs,

OINK! OINK!

and right past the dog.

WOOF! WOOF!

Then as the cat
    chased after Raggety-Taggle . . .

    . . . the dog chased after the cat . . .

MIAOW!

. . . followed by the cows, **Moo!**

then the sheep, **Ba**a-baaaa!

the horses, **Neigh!**

the pigs, **Oink! Oink!**

with the cockerel flapping behind . . .

Cock-a-doodle-do!

Raggety-Taggle nibbled peacefully
and wondered just why **anybody**
would **ever** want to make
a noise **at all.**

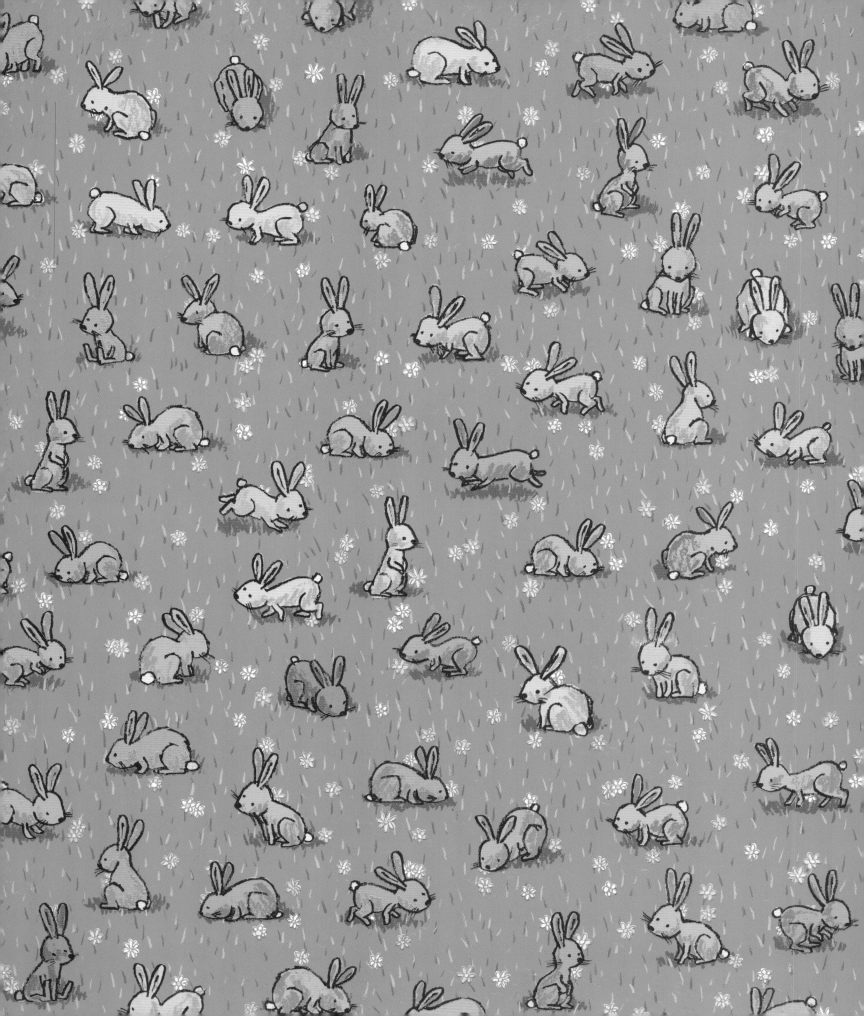